Cover removed @ REE/WC/ 2018

ONLY ONE COWRY

A DAHOMEAN TALE

retold by
PHILLIS GERSHATOR

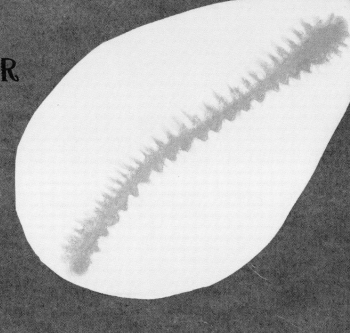

illustrated by
DAVID SOMAN

ORCHARD BOOKS   NEW YORK

THE FIRST KING OF DAHOMEY called his people together.

"I, Dada Segbo, am ready to marry," he announced.

His people were happy to hear it and gave him advice: "To find a wife, the king must give gifts to a young woman's family."

"Gifts?" asked the king, not wanting to part with his wealth. He held up one small cowry shell. "I have a gift. Here it is."

"No, no, no," protested his people. "Certainly the king knows that is not a good gift. One cowry is barely worth a bit of flint."

But a clever young fellow named Yo spoke up. "I will find the king a wife for only one cowry."

Dada Segbo gladly gave Yo the cowry shell to find him a wife.

With the cowry shell, Yo bought a bit of flint. Then, with the flint, he set a stack of straw on fire. Grasshoppers jumped out of the straw and into his sack.

"Grasshoppers for flint," Yo said, congratulating himself. "Well, well, I'm doing well, thanks to Dada Segbo's shell."

With a sack full of grasshoppers, Yo set off down the road to find a wife for the king.

Beans for grasshoppers.
Grasshoppers for flint.
Well, well, I'm doing well,
thanks to
Dada Segbo's shell.

On the way, he came to the house of an old woman. She was drying beans outside, but when she turned her back, hungry chickens snuck up behind her and pecked at the beans.

"Don't you have any chicken feed for your chickens?" asked Yo.

"No," said the woman.

"I will give your chickens some grasshoppers," Yo said.

Her chickens ate the grasshoppers and left the beans alone. And for his good deed, the woman offered Yo a sack full of beans.

Yo continued on his way with two sacks, congratulating himself:

When Yo crossed the river, he saw fishermen
fishing, but the fish weren't jumping.

"Watch this," Yo said to the fishermen.
"I will throw some beans into the river."

All the fish jumped for the beans. The
fishermen caught so many fish, they gave
Yo a sack full.

Yo went on his way with three sacks,
congratulating himself:

Fish for beans.
Beans for grasshoppers.
Grasshoppers for flint.
Well, well, I'm doing well,
thanks to
Dada Segbo's shell.

Farther down the road, Yo saw a blacksmith surrounded by half finished axes and knives.

Yo said, "You must be tired and hungry. I will cook a fish for you. And one for me, too, while I'm at it." Yo was always ready to eat.

After lunch the blacksmith, feeling strong again, finished his work, and, grateful for the food and company, he gave Yo a sack full of tools.

Yo continued on his way with four sacks, congratulating himself:

Tools for fish.
Fish for beans.
Beans for grasshoppers.
Grasshoppers for flint.
Well, well, I'm doing well,
thanks to Dada Segbo's shell.

"But not well enough," said Yo. "Not yet." And he stopped to watch a farmer clearing the land. The farmer's work was slow and hard.

"Your work will go faster if you use tools," Yo said, offering the farmer a knife and an ax.

In exchange the farmer gave Yo a jug of palm oil and a sack full of flour.

Yo continued on his way with five sacks and a jug, congratulating himself:

Oil for tools.
Tools for fish.
Fish for beans.
Beans for grasshoppers.
Grasshoppers for flint.
Well, well, I'm doing well,
thanks to
Dada Segbo's shell.

Yo reached a village next. There he saw a baker, but she had no bread to sell.

"Where is your bread?" asked Yo.

"I ran out of oil," she said. "I can't bake without oil."

Yo knew what to do. "You can have half of mine."

With half a jug of oil, the baker made a pile of corn bread.

She knew what to do too. She gave Yo a sack full.

Yo continued on his way with
six sacks and half a jug of oil,
congratulating himself:

Bread for oil.
Oil for tools.
Tools for fish.
Fish for beans.
Beans for grasshoppers.
Grasshoppers for flint.
Well, well, I'm doing well,
thanks to Dada Segbo's shell.

At last, with all these fine gifts, Yo was ready to find a wife for Dada Segbo.

In a commanding voice, he announced himself to the chief of the village.
"The messenger of Dada Segbo has come. He brings gifts to the chief. The
king asks that the chief's daughter become his wife."

The chief's daughter was very proud and pleased. The king had sent so
many gifts to her father! Bread, oil, tools . . .

She was prepared to return with Yo to the king's compound—until she overheard him tell a villager, "Go now and let the king know I have found him a beautiful wife for only one cowry."

"Only one cowry?" the chief's daughter asked Yo. "What do you mean?"
And Yo answered, "Dada Segbo gave me a cowry to find him a wife.
So I gave your father gifts:

Corn bread from the baker for half a jug of palm oil.
Oil and flour from the farmer for an ax and a knife.
Tools from the blacksmith who ate my fish for dinner.
Fish from the fishermen whose fish ate my beans.
Beans from the old woman whose chickens ate my grasshoppers.
Grasshoppers from the straw I burned with flint—
the flint I bought with Dada Segbo's cowry."

Oh, no, the chief's daughter thought. *This is not the end of it.* For she was not only beautiful. She was as clever as Yo, perhaps more so.

She told Yo, "Tell your messenger I cannot travel yet. I must eat before I leave. And please make sure the king's cooks prepare the kinds of food I like."

Yo understood perfectly. He told the messenger, "Tell the king to send us food before we leave and to prepare a variety of dishes, because the future queen is fussy about what she eats. Oh, and don't forget to say, 'She's very hungry, so send a lot.'"

Dada Segbo was delighted to receive the news that he was to have a wife for only one cowry, and he immediately ordered his cooks to prepare food for her. He sent fifty big calabashes filled with sweet and spicy meats, squash, sauce, rice, and yams to the chief's house. There was so much food, the whole village feasted day and night.

Afterward the chief's daughter said to Yo, "The food was good, but the king did not send anything to drink, and now I am thirsty."

Yo sent a messenger to tell the king they needed something to drink. "Tell him to send palm wine," Yo said. "Oh, and don't forget to say, 'Send a lot. The future queen is very, very thirsty.'"

Dada Segbo, who had found a wife for only one cowry, could do no less than send one hundred calabashes of palm wine to the chief's house. There was enough palm wine for everyone in the village, including Yo.

After the festivities the future queen told Yo, "The drink was good, but how can I travel without new clothes? I wouldn't want to disgrace the king."

Yo sent a messenger to tell the king that the future queen and Yo, his faithful servant, needed new clothes so as not to disgrace Dada Segbo upon their arrival.

Of course, Dada Segbo didn't want his wife—
or his servant—to look poor and shabby. He sent
a trunk of fine cloths and jewelry to the chief's
house—and a handsome robe to Yo.

The chief's daughter, it is true, would have been beautiful dressed only in raffia, but how magnificent she was now, wrapped in the most elegant cloths. And she chose to wear, of all the jewelry that Dada Segbo sent, not the gold and precious beads, but the necklaces and bracelets made of shiny, brightly colored cowries. *Hundreds* of cowries.

"Now," she told Yo, "I am ready to marry the king."

From that day on, Dada Segbo couldn't stop marveling at his luck in finding such a wonderful wife, a woman like no other. "Only one cowry! Only one cowry!" he gloated, and he gladly rewarded Yo—with *another* cowry.

Yo bought a sweet potato with the shiny shell.

Congratulating himself on his cleverness, he dug a hole in the ground and said, "Well, well, I'm doing well, thanks to Dada Segbo's shell. . . ."

But that is another story.

Author's Note

When a couple marries in any culture, it's a time of celebration. Gifts are exchanged in one form or another—money, labor, drink, food, property, cloth. In Africa the family of the groom traditionally offers these kinds of gifts, called bride-price or bride-wealth, to the family of the bride.

For four thousand years, cowry shells were used as money. When they first appeared in Africa, they were so valuable that two cowries could serve as the bride-price. Later that number rose to ten thousand. Still later, at the end of the 1800s, when cowries lost value as traders flooded the market with them, the number rose to one hundred thousand.

Only One Cowry is freely based on two versions of "Profitable Amends: A Wife for One Cowry" in Melville Herskovits' collection, *Dahomean Narrative* (Evanston, Ill.: Northwestern University Press, 1958). In these twentieth-century versions told to Herskovits, Yo is a greedy and unscrupulous trickster. In the second of the two, the king, happy with his wife, forbids anyone to complain about Yo's trickery. According to the storyteller, that explains why Yo becomes a likable hero in future funny tales, as I prefer to picture him in this retelling for the twenty-first century.

To my father, Morton, my husband, David, and my editor, Sarah Caguiat—P.G.

To Matt, Claudia, Isa, and Sadie—D.S.

Thanks to Joshua Dimondstein, managing director, Dimondstein Tribal Arts, and Elisabeth Cameron, curator of African Art, The Nelson-Atkins Museum, for sharing their time and their knowledge of West African cultures.

Orchard Books, A Grolier Company,
95 Madison Avenue, New York, NY 10016

Manufactured in the United States of America. Printed and bound by Phoenix Color Corp. Book design by Mina Greenstein. The text of this book is set in 14 point Veljovic Medium. The illustrations are collage.
10 9 8 7 6 5 4 3 2 1

Library of Congress Cataloging-in-Publication Data
Gershator, Phillis.
Only one cowry : a Dahomean tale / retold by Phillis Gershator ; illustrated by David Soman.
p. cm.
Summary: A clever young fellow persuades an equally clever chief's daughter to marry the king of Dahomey, and both the young man and future queen prosper in the bargain.
ISBN 0-531-30288-1 (tr. : alk. paper)
ISBN 0-531-33288-8 (lib. bdg. : alk. paper)
[1. Folklore—Benin.] I. Soman, David, ill. II. Title.
PZ8.1.G353 On 2000 398.2'096683—dc21 [E]
99-56552